MR. NOISY
The Musician

Roger Hargreaves

MR. MEN   LITTLE MISS

MR. MEN™ LITTLE MISS™ © THOIP (a SANRIO company)

Mr Noisy The Musician © 2014 THOIP (a SANRIO company)
Printed and published under licence from Price Stern Sloan, Inc., Los Angeles.
First published in France 1997 by Hachette Livre
This edition published in 2014 by Dean, an imprint of Egmont UK Limited,
The Yellow Building, 1 Nicholas Road, London W11 4AN

ISBN 978 0 6035 6994 4
58234/2
Printed in Great Britain

EGMONT

On this particular morning, a van was driving through the town. It was going towards Mr Noisy's house. The van belonged to Mr Music, the musical instrument seller.

And what was in his van?

Musical instruments of course!

But which ones?

Well, you know Mr Noisy, so you can probably guess …

"WONDERFUL!" cried Mr Noisy when he saw the van arriving. "Here are my musical instruments. I've always loved making a noise. Sometimes people find me too loud but now that I'm going to be a real musician everyone will be so pleased."

Mr Noisy rushed to help Mr Music unload his van.

"Goodbye and THANK YOU," boomed Mr Noisy,
a little later, as the van drove away.

PAH! RUM! CRASH! CRASH!

What was the mysterious instrument that was making Mr Noisy's house shake from top to bottom?

And ...

… that was forcing Little Miss Star to close all her windows to shut out the terrible din?

What was the musical instrument that was …

… making Mr Grumble grumble a great deal?

Yes. Mr Noisy had a drum kit. A very big and very loud drum kit.

Mr Noisy's neighbours were not at all pleased. And Mr Uppity, who certainly didn't mind speaking his mind, went to call on Mr Noisy.

"Tell me," he demanded, "when are you going to stop deafening us? We've all had enough of your terrible din!"

"Din?" repeated Mr Noisy, most surprised. "My music? A din? I was hoping to please you all."

Mr Noisy certainly did not want to upset his neighbours, so he asked Mr Music to swap his drum kit for a less noisy instrument.

STRUM! STRUM! TWANG!

Mr Noisy's house certainly didn't sound much quieter.

Can you work out what the new instrument was?

Whatever the instrument was, it certainly made a lot of noise!

Little Miss Splendid wasn't able to get any beauty sleep, so she decided to pay Mr Noisy a visit in the morning.

"Mr Noisy," she said, sharply. "Take a good look at me. Tell me where have my fair complexion and my bright eyes gone? I'm missing my beauty sleep!"

"You like my music so much that you can't sleep at night?" asked Mr Noisy. "I'm so pleased. Do come in and I'll play you a little tune."

But no, Little Miss Splendid did not like Mr Noisy's guitar music. Yes, that's right. It was a guitar.

And Mr Noisy, who was hoping to become a famous pop star, was most disappointed.

On her way home, Little Miss Splendid met Mr Clever.

"My ears are going to explode," she complained.
"My face is pale and I have bags under my eyes.
And all because of Mr Noisy's noise. It's outrageous!"

But, Mr Clever had an idea ...

… an idea that Mr Noisy liked very much indeed.

The next day was a day to celebrate.

Not simply because the terrible din had stopped but also because an orchestra had arrived in town and they were playing wonderful music.

And the conductor was … none other than Mr Noisy, who waved his baton in time to the music …

… in silence!